BUNNY
the Brave
WAR HORSE
BASED ON A TRUE STORY

Elizabeth MacLeod   Marie Lafrance

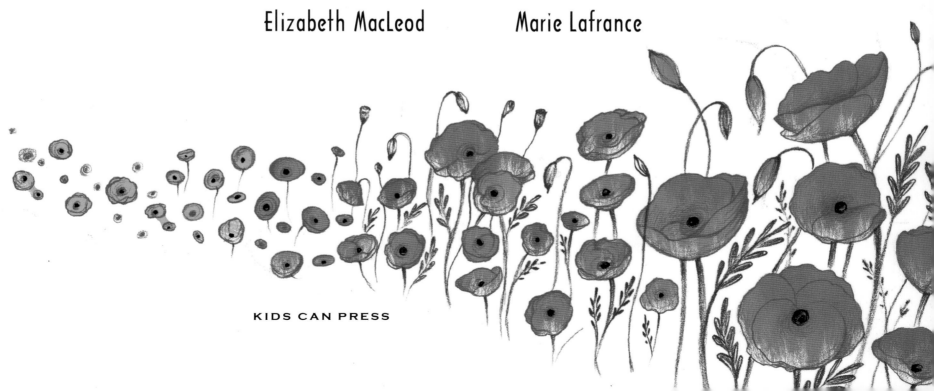

KIDS CAN PRESS

"Atten-TION!"

The police officers sat tall in their saddles. Their uniforms were spotless. Their buttons gleamed in the bright August sun.

But no one was really looking at the officers. Instead, an army major was choosing the best horses. Just a few weeks earlier, a war had started across the ocean in Europe. The major needed horses for his soldiers to ride.

Even the horses seemed to realize it was a special moment. They stood perfectly still. Their ears were alert, and their eyes were shining.

"I want all of these here," the major said, pointing to a group of horses. "And, of course, this magnificent one." The major was standing in front of a handsome, reddish-brown horse. "What is his name?" he asked the police officer sitting high on the horse's back.

"We call him Bunny, sir," said the officer, Thomas Dundas.

"Bunny?" The major laughed. "That's an odd name for a horse."

"It's because of his ears, sir," said Tom. "You can see they're a little long. You know, like a bunny's. But he's brave as a tiger, sir."

Bunny and many other horses were sent by ship across the Atlantic Ocean to Europe.

There were lots of soldiers on the ship, too. Tom and his brother, "Bud," were there. They had both joined the army to fight overseas.

Tom was glad when Bud was given Bunny to ride. Tom knew what a good horse Bunny was.

It was late winter by the time the soldiers and horses arrived in France. From there, they traveled to Belgium, where they joined the fighting.

Their first day of battle would be one they'd never forget.

Bud and Bunny rode toward the fighting. So did Tom and his horse.

Suddenly they saw a strange, yellowy-green cloud. It crept forward over the ground. Then the brothers heard the soldiers in front yelling.

"My throat! I can't breathe!"

"I can't see!"

"It's gas, men!" shouted a major. "Poison gas!"

There had never been an attack like this before. Horses were neighing and squealing. The gas was burning their eyes and throats, too.

It was many hours before the wind blew the gas away.

Bunny and the other war horses helped the soldiers in many important ways.

If messages needed to be delivered quickly, the horses galloped as fast as they could.

Bunny sometimes carried wounded soldiers off the battlefield. Bud would lift the men onto Bunny's strong back.

Some horses pulled ambulances and carts loaded with supplies. When the carts were full of food, the soldiers were very happy to see them!

Horses also hauled cannons and other big, heavy guns onto the battlefield.

Bud and Bunny worked hard on the battlefield, as well.

During one battle, it was only noon but the sky was midnight black. Drenching rain and thick smoke from the guns made it almost impossible to see.

Bombs exploded all around. The noise was terrifying. Bud felt Bunny tremble but the horse didn't try to run away. He was a trained police horse.

"That's it, Bunny," Bud said, as they charged forward. "We'll both pretend to be brave."

Guns thundered and grenades boomed.

At dinnertime that day, Tom looked for Bud so they could eat together. But another soldier stopped him.

"The captain wants to see you. Right away."

Tom headed to the captain's office.

"I'm afraid I've got some bad news, Tom. Very bad news. Your brother died in battle today."

Tom stared at the captain. He couldn't say a word.

"Bud was a brave soldier," said the captain. "You should be proud of him."

After a moment, the captain spoke again. "I'd like you to ride Bud's horse. I believe his name is Bunny."

Dazed, Tom stumbled out of the captain's office. He hardly saw the soldiers around him. Tom just kept walking and walking. He finally ended up in the stable with Bunny and the other horses.

"Well, Bunny," said Tom sadly, "we're going to have to do our best without Bud. It's just you and me now."

Tom hugged Bunny's neck. Bunny whinnied quietly. He gently nibbled on Tom's hair.

Rain poured down for weeks on end. It turned the roads
to mud. Few wagons of food could reach the soldiers. The
men had almost nothing to eat. Neither did the horses.

Tom visited Bunny in the stable one night. He noticed that the
horse beside Bunny was shivering. The horse had been so hungry
it had eaten its blanket.

"All I've got for you is this handful of oats, Bunny," Tom said.
"I know you're hungry. So am I."

Tom rubbed his horse's nose. "Poor Bunny," he whispered.
"I chose to come here and fight. No one gave you a choice."

Days later, Tom woke up with the sun on his face. The rain had finally stopped!

Tom whistled as he brushed Bunny later that morning.

"Captain wants you to take a message to headquarters right quick," another soldier told him.

"Will do!" said Tom, fastening Bunny's saddle.

Tom and Bunny trotted out into the sunshine. Bunny neighed and tossed his head. On either side of the road, poppies glowed brilliant red in the sun.

"You know, Bunny," said Tom, "I bet this is a beautiful place when there's no war going on."

On the way home, Tom and Bunny saw some soldiers at the side of the road. In the ditch was a large cart.

"Our horse ran away! Then the cart slipped off the road," said one of the men. "We can't move it."

"The enemy is getting closer," said another soldier anxiously. "We've got to get out of here!"

"I'm sure my horse, Bunny, can help," Tom said, jumping down out of the saddle.

"I doubt a horse named Bunny can be much use," said a tall, thin soldier with a sneer.

But the other soldiers helped Tom hitch Bunny to the heavy cart.

"Pull, Bunny! PULL!" shouted the soldiers. With a groan,
Bunny tried to move forward. But his hooves slipped in the mud.
A bullet whistled just over Tom's head. Two more hit the cart.

"Come on, Bunny," Tom whispered in his ear. "I know you can
do it."

Bunny tried again. He pulled with all his might. Slowly, the cart
began to move. The soldiers cheered as Bunny trudged forward.

"That's some horse you've got," the skinny soldier said with
admiration.

"The best," said Tom proudly. "Now, let's keep moving!"

On November 11, 1918, Tom raced into Bunny's stable.

"Bunny! Bunny! It's over!" yelled Tom. "The war is over!
We won! We can go home!"

Soldiers cheered. Bells clanged. People sang and shouted.
After more than four years, there was finally peace again.

Tom hugged his horse's neck. "We made it. We survived."

Then Tom whispered, "If only Bud were here with us."

Bunny whinnied quietly. He gently nibbled on Tom's hair.

Tom sailed home a few weeks later. No officer on his police
force had earned more medals in the war than he did. Maybe that
was because no other policeman had a horse like Bunny.

Tom's police force had sent eighteen horses to help in the war.
Of all those horses, Bunny was the only one alive at the end. He
did not return home with Tom, though. Like most horses that
survived the war, he was sold to farmers in Belgium.

But Tom never forgot Bunny, the brave war horse.

Bunny, Bud, Tom and WWI

World War I began on July 28, 1914, after years of uneasiness and conflict in Europe. The war pitted the Allies (including Canada, France, the United Kingdom — you can see a portrait of its king at the time, George V, on page 14 — Russia and later the United States and Italy) against the Central Powers of Germany and Austria-Hungary. Most of the fighting took place in Belgium and northern France, but there were also battles in Africa, Asia, the Pacific and more.

The mounted police force of Toronto, Ontario, Canada, sent four officers and eighteen horses, including Bunny, to fight in the 9th Battery Canadian Field Artillery. Constable Thomas H. Dundas was one of those police officers. His brother served in the same battery. There are no records telling us this brother's name — he's been given the nickname "Bud" for this story.

Going to War

Bunny, Bud, Tom and the other soldiers and horses in the 9th Battery headed across the Atlantic Ocean on October 3, 1914. They arrived in England during one of Europe's coldest winters.

The 9th Battery sailed to France a few months later, and then headed to Ypres, Belgium. They were on the front lines of battle on April 22, 1915, when the Germans launched the war's first gas attack. (Days later, Canadian Dr. John McCrae wrote the famous war poem "In Flanders Fields.") By the end of April, few of the police horses that had been shipped over with Bunny were still alive.

Horses in War

Unlike in previous wars, during World War I there weren't a lot of cavalry charges, with the soldiers on both sides rushing at each other on horseback. But horses were still very important. They could travel through mud and rough terrain better than cars and trucks. Horses carried messengers and soldiers who were scouting out enemy positions.

These brave animals also pulled artillery, ambulances and supply wagons. They boosted morale among the soldiers, too. Some people estimate that more than eight million horses served in World War I for both sides.

The horses and their riders often had to go without food. Either the supplies couldn't get to them or the food went bad. Horses ate anything they could — even blankets, the epaulets on soldiers' shoulders and candles!

Bunny and Tom served in many important battles the Canadian forces fought, including two of the most well-known: the Battle of the Somme in 1916, and the Battle of Vimy Ridge in 1917.

The War Ends
World War I ended on November 11, 1918.

Bunny and Tom were in Mons, Belgium, when they received the news that the Allies had defeated the Central Powers. Sergeant-Major Thomas Dundas returned home a hero.

Most horses from Britain, Canada and the United States were sold to farmers in Belgium and France and never saw their homes again. Tom and the city of Toronto tried to bring Bunny back. But by the time enough money was raised to transport him, Bunny had already been sold and couldn't be found.

Next November 11, think about the service and sacrifice of all brave soldiers. And don't forget about courageous horses like Bunny.

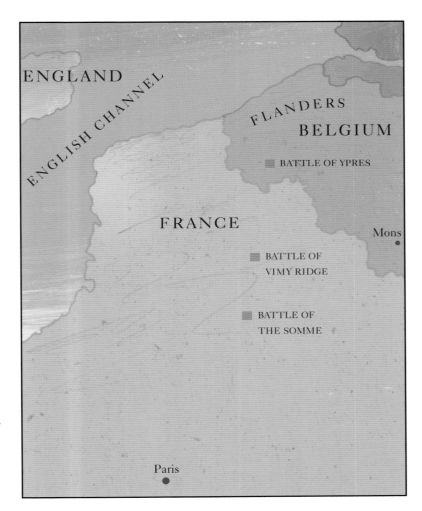

Bunny, Bud and Tom fought for the Allies in Belgium and France

With thanks and admiration to the students and staff of Monsignor O'Donoghue
Catholic Elementary School, especially librarian Lisa Kennedy Hiltz — E.M.

To belle-maman Louise McGovern Dubuc, whose father, Captain William Frank McGovern,
Military Cross and Bar, fought in World War I — M.L.

ACKNOWLEDGMENTS

I am very grateful to my consultants: Dr. Mélanie Morin-Pelletier, Historian, First World War, Canadian War Museum;
and Staff-Inspector William Wardle, Unit Commander, Toronto Police Mounted, Police Dog and Marine Units.
They were both so generous with their time and knowledge. I really appreciate their involvement and interest in this project.

Many thanks also to librarian Lara Andrews and all the staff at the Military History Research Centre, Canadian War Museum;
Alix McEwen, Reference Archivist, Library and Archives Canada; and Richard Sanderson, Director, Naval Museum of Halifax, Nova Scotia.

Special thanks to Stacey Roderick, who earned many "Best Editor Ever" points during the creation of this book! Many thanks to
illustrator Marie Lafrance for bringing Bunny's story to life and to art director Marie Bartholomew for yet another beautifully
designed book. Thanks also to editor Karen Li.

Thanks always to my dad, a brave veteran of World War II, and my brothers, John and Douglas.
And very special thanks to Paul, who's always at my side through all of life's battles.

Kids Can Press acknowledges the financial support of the Government of
Ontario, through the Ontario Media Development Corporation's Ontario
Book Initiative; the Ontario Arts Council; the Canada Council for the Arts;
and the Government of Canada, through the CBF, for our publishing activity.

Published in Canada by
Kids Can Press Ltd.
25 Dockside Drive
Toronto, ON M5A 0B5

www.kidscanpress.com

Published in the U.S. by
Kids Can Press Ltd.
2250 Military Road
Tonawanda, NY 14150

The artwork in this book was rendered in mixed media and Photoshop.
The text is set in Caslon.

Edited by Stacey Roderick
Designed by Marie Bartholomew

This book is smyth sewn casebound.
Manufactured in Tseung Kwan O, NT Hong Kong, China, in 3/2014
by Paramount Printing Co. Ltd.

CM 14 0 9 8 7 6 5 4 3 2 1

Library and Archives Canada Cataloguing in Publication

MacLeod, Elizabeth, author

    Bunny the brave war horse : based on a true story / written
by Elizabeth MacLeod ; illustrated by Marie Lafrance.

ISBN 978-1-77138-024-9 (bound)

    1. War horses — Juvenile fiction. 2. World War, 1914–1918 —
Juvenile fiction. I. Lafrance, Marie, illustrator II. Title.

PS8575.L4608B86 2014   jC813'.54   C2013-908244-1

Kids Can Press is a lORUS™ Entertainment company